THE HUNGER HEROES

Missed Meal Mayhem

BY JARRETT LERNER

Aladdin

NEW YORK   LONDON   TORONTO   SYDNEY   NEW DELHI

In a seemingly ordinary city...

Atop a seemingly ordinary building...

Live a group of EXTRAordinary heroes...

ALADDIN / An imprint of Simon & Schuster Children's Publishing Division / 1230 Avenue of the Americas, New York, New York 10020 / First Aladdin edition October 2021 / Copyright © 2021 by Jarrett Lerner / All rights reserved, including the right of reproduction in whole or in part in any form. / ALADDIN and related logo are registered trademarks of Simon & Schuster, Inc. / For information about special discounts for bulk purchases, please contact Simon & Schuster Special Sales at 1-866-506-1949 or business@simonandschuster.com. / The Simon & Schuster Speakers Bureau can bring authors to your live event. For more information or to book an event contact the Simon & Schuster Speakers Bureau at 1-866-248-3049 or visit our website at www.simonspeakers.com. / Designed by Jarrett Lerner & Karin Paprocki / The illustrations for this book were rendered digitally. / The text of this book was hand-lettered. / Manufactured in China 0721 SCP / 10 9 8 7 6 5 4 3 2 1 / Library of Congress Control Number 2021931258 / ISBN 9781534462823 (hc) / ISBN 9781534462809 (pbk) / ISBN 9781534462816 (ebook)

For Myrsini Stephanides

The Hunger Heroes are superpowered taco ingredients who help the kids of their city whenever they need a snack!

Just look at these happy campers!

Next up, there's

CHIP NINJA!

She's crafty!

She's clever!

She's 100% CORN BASED!

And wait till you see her GADGETS!

WOW!

NEAT!

FANCY!

And last but not least...

Leonard?

Where's Leonard?

CHAPTER 1

It was a regular Tuesday morning at Hunger Heroes headquarters.

an alarm sounded!

Tammy tossed aside her weights and hurried over to the report machine. As she read the report, her expression turned grim.

"It's a missed meal," Chip Ninja said.

She snatched the report out of Tammy's hand and looked it over herself.

Some kid is sitting in school without any breakfast in his belly.

10-29

Missed Meal: Breakfast

NAME: Jason

LOCATION: Pinchkid Elementary School—Mrs. Sternbladder's Classroom

LAST MEAL: Mac and cheese; half-bowl; 5:35 p.m. yesterday

ENERGY LEVEL: Lower than low

CONCENTRATION: Nonexistent

ADDITIONAL INFO: Math test at approximately 11:15 a.m. (pre-lunchtime)

There was no time to lose.

The Hunger Heroes had to get to the school—and FAST!

CHAPTER 2

The Hunger Heroes Hovercraft soared through the sky toward James H. Pinchkid Elementary School.

BARF BAG

VOMIT VAT

PUKE BUCKET

Poor kid must be starved.

He'll fail that test if he doesn't get a snack.

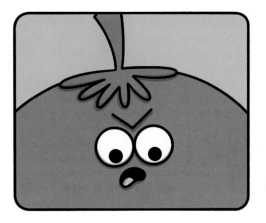

"Well," Tammy said, "we know he won't be getting any snacks from Mrs. Sternbladder...."

8-95

Adult ID Report

NAME: Susannah Sternbladder

OCCUPATION: Educator

ADDITIONAL INFO: Despiser of snacks; crusader against crumbs

WISE WORDS
ALERT!

"Now, Tammy," cautioned Mr. Toots. "We shouldn't be so quick to judge Mrs. Sternbladder. There's always more to someone's story than meets the eye."

"For all we know, we could help two people today—Jason AND Mrs. Sternbladder."

STEP 1

THE OL'
RAZZLE-

CHAPTER 3

The Hunger Heroes made it to the school in record time. Tammy lowered the Hovercraft and landed on the lawn.

Welp, we tried. We gave it our all. But it says right there: door's locked. Guess there's nothing for us to do but head home.

Leonard! You know we could never do that! Not with that boy in there in need of a snack.

Lunchtime isn't for hours, and he has a TEST!

I'll get us inside.

Follow me.

Chip Ninja led the others around to the side of the building until she found what she was looking for.

CHAPTER 4

Perched on the windowsill, the Hunger Heroes found themselves looking in on something entirely unexpected.

For the first time in a long time, the Hunger Heroes were baffled about what their next step should be.

"Should we look for a different way into the school?" Tammy asked.

Leonard nodded.

But Chip Ninja nixed that suggestion just a second later.

"There's no time," she said. "Jason needs us NOW."

51

The dodgeballs came fast and furious.

But the superheroic foursome had survived their fair share of danger.

And so the Hunger Heroes darted and dodged. They ducked and dove. They punched and punted and swatted and charged.

Step-by-step, they made their way across the gym.

59

CHAPTER 4½

As you can see, Mrs. Sternbladder had a lot of rules. Most of them had to do with NOT EATING.

Mrs. Sternbladder couldn't stand snacks. She couldn't stand the sounds of chewing and munching. She couldn't even stand the little noises of nibbling!

Her room was a NO-SNACK ZONE. And if she caught you creating crumbs...well, LOOK OUT.

Inside her classroom, Mrs. Sternbladder had just begun discussing the upcoming math test.

Mrs. Sternbladder's words reached Jason's ears but didn't make it into his brain. As he drifted off, so did his thoughts....

CHAPTER 5

The Hunger Heroes roamed up and down the halls of the school, searching for Mrs. Sternbladder's classroom. But it was proving very difficult to find.

This place is a maze....

71

CHAPTER 6

The Hunger Heroes ran as fast as they could, but they couldn't seem to escape the angry buzz of the vacuum cleaner.

Mr. Toots slowed to a stop. Then, as the rest of the Hunger Heroes caught up, he quickly reviewed the steps of the Ol' Razzle-Dazzle.

There, there, Leonard. No one's going to the Great Taco Shop in the Sky. Not today. Not on my watch.

"We just need a distraction," Chip Ninja said. "Something to get Mrs. Sternbladder out of her classroom so we can get Jason an Emergency Snack."

The Hunger Heroes looked around the hallway.

"You want a distraction?" said Tammy. "I'll give you a distraction!"

Mrs. Sternbladder didn't see anything odd right outside her classroom, so she headed down the hall.

CHAPTER 7

The Hunger Heroes stood at the front of the classroom and searched the sea of faces before them.

STERNBLADDER

You are within a

NO-SNACK ZONE

At last, Mr. Toots spotted Jason.

He was all the way at the back of the room, and looking worse than ever.

97

It was a moment the Hunger Heroes would never forget.

Chip Ninja, unprepared? Impossible!

Leonard held the salt cracker out to Chip Ninja.

She grabbed it, then strapped on her Bouncy Boots and rushed toward Jason.

103

Two plus four times nine minus sixteen divided by eleven plus one hundred five times two times two hundred minus eight plus six mi... ...ur equals 42,018.5455!

CORRECT!

The next chapter may cause you to **EMPATHIZE*** with an **ADULT.**

*To understand and share the feelings of someone else.

CHAPTER 8

Mrs. Sternbladder stomped into her classroom.

She glared at the Hunger Heroes. Then she glared at the cracker crumbs on Jason's desk....

And then she went from upset
to furious!

What were the Hunger Heroes to do?

They could make a run for it....

But then they would be leaving Jason and all the other kids to deal with Mrs. Sternbladder all alone.

And that wouldn't be very heroic....

Which was why Mr. Toots finally stepped forward.

"There is," Mrs. Sternbladder told Mr. Toots.

She took a deep breath and told her students a story....

It all started when I was a kid, going to a school much like this one.

One day during class, I got a little hungry. My stomach was growling so loudly that I was having trouble focusing. So... I snuck a few bites of a snack.

Well, I must have dropped some crumbs, because the next thing I knew, there were ants everywhere!

119

All at once the Heroes remembered that Tammy was still out in the hallway—and so was THE VACUUM! They scurried out of the classroom to find her.

Mr. Toots flew himself and his friends closer and closer to the vacuum.

"Get ready!" he called to Chip Ninja and Leonard. "I'm about to run out of gas!"

And not a second after the words had left the big bean's lips... the Heroes fell.

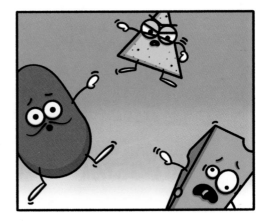

Fortunately, they fell right onto the vacuum cleaner and...

Nice of you three to join me. And right on time. Here's the door!

burst through the door of the school
and back outside.

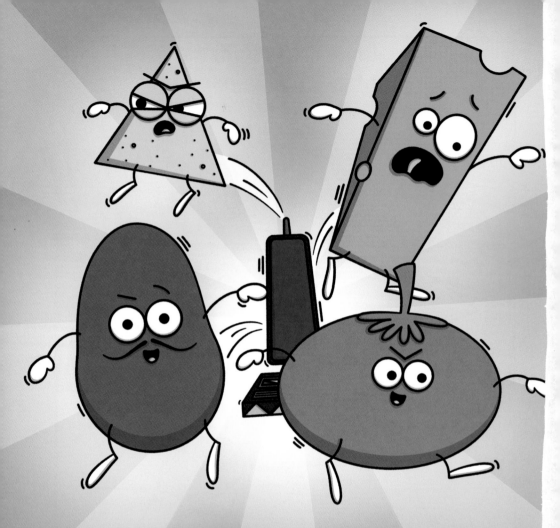

Leaping off the vacuum, the Hunger Heroes hurried to the Hovercraft, ready for their next adventure!